THE SEVEN WIVES OF SILVER

BOOKS BY CLARK

THE STAINS OF TIME

The Piano of Death

The Boot of Destiny

The Chains of Desire

The Elixir of Denial

The Dance of Dreams

OTHER BOOKS

Those Little Bastards

All He Left Behind

Missing Mr. Wingfield

The Seven Wives of Silver

Bad Poetry Night

Out of the Woods

Under the World

THE SEVEN WIVES OF SILVER

E. CHRISTOPHER CLARK

Published in the United States by Clarkwoods in Chelmsford, Massachusetts.

This is a work of fiction. Names, characters, places, and incidents either are the product of the author's imagination or are used fictitiously, and any resemblance to any actual persons, living or dead, events, or locales is entirely coincidental.

ISBN for the Print Edition: 978-1-952044-07-6
ISBN for the Digital Edition: 978-0-9994044-5-4

Library of Congress Control Number: 2018913216

PREFACE

This book contains some of the best stuff I wrote in my 30s, but it also contains problematic elements I would not use in my writing today.

I wrote the first bits of what would become *The Seven Wives of Silver* for a pair of pulpy, provocative anthologies, and everything else followed from there. That said, in my desire to shock audiences with the horrors faced by Silas Silver, his sister, and his seven wives, I made a few questionable choices.

I have considered pulling this book from publication altogether, but the Internet never truly lets something disappear. And so, I've done what I can to lessen any hurt the book might inadvertently cause by adding this brief preface and the following mea culpas:

- "Cacophony" includes a depiction of brother-sister incest. I was watching too much *Game of Thrones* at the time, I guess, and trying too hard to emulate it. What I regret most here is that the story would've worked just fine *without* the incest. It might have even worked better.

- Sexual violence is also pervasive throughout the rest of the book. And while I still believe some of it serves the story, the book would certainly have benefited from more rounds of beta-reading.

Thank you for taking the time to read this preface. I hope, despite these issues, you can still enjoy the shocking lives of Silas Silver, his sister Sarah, and his wives. I think there's good stuff in here. Just be careful and put it down for a while if you need to.

E. Christopher Clark
Chelmsford, Massachusetts
December 14, 2023

CONTENTS

1. Cacophony   1
2. The Boot   4
3. Animals   17
4. The Patience for Taming   23
5. The Charity of Ruin   28
6. The Best Thing for Both of Us   35
7. The Whore of Harwich   42
8. The Crone on the Common   56
9. One Last Bounty   68

Acknowledgements   71
About the Author   73

For the many wives of my great-grandfather, Charles Clark (1889-1956), and for all his descendants, in the hopes that he wasn't half as bad as his on-page counterpart turned out to be

When you're brought into this world,
    they say you're born in sin.
    Well, at least they gave me something
    I didn't have to steal or have to win.

THE SEVEN WIVES OF SILVER

CACOPHONY

1864

You wake to the wailing of your mother, the cacophony of her latter days stirring you from the deepest slumber of your life. You reach across your bed to take your brother's hand in your own, to give him the courage he needs these days to open his eyes, but he's gone.

Fine then, you think. Here's a chance to take care of yourself, for once. You reach between your legs, to that place where his absence is most obvious, and you rest your warm hand there to wish the soreness away, But it's then, right at that moment, that you hear the first gunshot.

And then the second, and the third. And so on.

They're coming from outside, you realize, as you burst from your bed and then through the door. But that doesn't slow you down. He may not be putting your mother out of her misery just yet, but chances are that Silas is still up to no good.

"You're indecent," is all he says to you as bound out onto the back lawn in nothing but the clothes God gave you.

It's dark but for the half-moon overhead and the curtains of stars that moon is peeking out from behind. The hedgerow between you and your only neighbor is high and the beach to the other side is vacant but for the gulls that call it home.

"What will Old Man Brown say?" asks your brother as he reloads the pistol.

"If he can see over the shrubbery," you say, "I'm sure he's too busy attending to himself to have words for us."

Silas smiles as he hands you the pistol. "You are no Tamson," he says, shaking his head.

"I know," you say, taking the gun from him. "I shared our cousin's bed more often than you did."

He says nothing for a moment and you can't read his face in the dark.

"I'm sorry," you say, and you are. Tamson is a sore spot for Silas and you shouldn't have poked him there.

"Practice," he says.

"Now?" you say. "At night? In my condition?" you add, with a smile and a sway of your hips.

High above the two of you, your mother screams the name of Silas. But whether she's calling for your brother or your long-dead father, you can't be sure.

"Practice," he says.

You take aim and fire and glass shatters across the way. You aim and fire, aim and fire. And when your bullets are spent, you hand the gun back to your brother and he tells you again that you're a natural—better than he's ever been.

"If only you'd had me at Secessionville," you tell him.

"I wouldn't have been the only one to have you," he says. "You may be a great shot, but soldiers are soldiers. Men are men."

He smiles, but you don't. You know all too well that men are men, even brothers. Even brothers whose faces are buried in books when they aren't buried between your thighs. Hadn't you said no, last night? Hadn't you said it again and again, that you were done, that you couldn't do this anymore? And hadn't he used your embrace as you wiped away his tears about your mother—

hadn't he used that as his excuse to turn no into maybe, maybe into yes, fine, okay, but be quick?

He hands you the gun again, having reloaded it once more. And this is when he tells you that he thought to bring the pistol upstairs, to put your mother out of her misery. Or, if not the gun, a knife. If not the knife, then a pillow.

"All because she's begged you to have a child?"

"I would have," he spits, and you know he's thinking of Tamson again. "I would have."

He asks you to hold your fire while he stalks across the lawn to reset the targets. And you do hold the gun at your side until his back is turned. But then you raise it—you raise the gun and point it straight at him. And you wonder if you should do it. You are a woman, after all. It'd be chalked up to an accident. And this is not the same boy that you, your mother, and your sisters sent off to war. Is he joking about what he'd do to your mother if courage finally found him? Maybe, but maybe not.

There are voices on the wind again, or maybe just in your head. Do it, they whisper. Do it. You count six of them this time, though you don't check behind you to make sure. Where is the seventh, you wonder. But then, there she is: begging for mercy. Begging for Silas, as she always does.

Above you, another scream rends the air. And so, you shush the voices that follow you these days and you lower the gun. Because right now—right now, you understand.

As he steps out of the darkness, tears in his eyes, you see the boy you helped raise. You see him and you forgive him, even if you shouldn't.

Even though you know, in your heart—in every bone in your body—that you should not. You. Should. Not.

THE BOOT

1892

Now that she'd scraped seven flakes from the sole of the boot, Ada set it back inside its box and set to wrapping her gift in the plain brown paper that Silas favored for parcels and presents both. She finished off the offering with a bow strung from simplest twine, set the package upon the table, and then leaned back with a sense of satisfaction into the ornate pillows with which she'd adorned her husband's modest divan.

Ada closed her eyes and breathed deep, taking heed of each inhale and exhale. Just as her mother had done, and her mother before her, and every mother back to the mother of them all. Thought was gone from her for a good long while before she found herself wondering if fortune would smile this night upon her well-laid plans. She sighed at the uncertainty, then leaned forward to take her tea cup from the table.

She sprinkled the flakes she had gathered from the boot into the concoction she had brewed with care for a fortnight. Then she stirred with a spoon stolen from her husband's finest set. Seven times to the left, seven to the right. Satisfied, she set the spoon down upon the saucer and began to sip.

When there was nothing left to drink, Ada turned the cup in her hand. And as she turned it, she spoke an incantation. "Oh dregs," she said, "I plead with all my might, please bring me what I need this night."

Wind ruffled the curtains of the home her husband had built for her here at the edge of the deep green sea, the home he'd built upon the spot where his forefathers had been building homes for the loves of their lives since time immemorial. Ada knew that Silas grew tired of the effort to make proud those dear departed souls who had begot him by finally begetting himself, but she would not give up. She knew that a parent's wishes—a mother's in particular—were a powerful magic. And so, as the chill of the wind made gooseflesh of her bare arms, she begged for guidance. "Cup," she said, "what say you?"

But the cup said nothing.

Panic stricken, Ada yanked her necklace from its hiding place within her bodice and began to twirl it over the cup. "Leaves of magic," she chanted, "leaves of must. Do not break our sacred trust."

Then she placed her hands gently upon her belly.

"Oh, womb," she whispered, "you home without a tenant—your walls will be filled this night, I promise you. Your chamber will be occupied at last!"

On the porch, quite suddenly, there were footsteps. With all due haste, Ada tidied her cup and saucer. Then she crossed quickly to the door, arriving just before it opened, and presented her cheek for her husband's kiss.

With his nose buried in some great tome as he crossed the threshold, he paid her no mind. But he must have noticed her there, for he made no move to close the door behind him. So Ada closed it herself and waited for him to finish.

She was standing there for at least few minutes more before he marked his page, slapped the book shut, and turned to face her.

"Did you know," he said, shaking the book in her general direction, "that Booth was an actor, dear? He played quite a bit of Shakespeare."

"I'm sorry," said Ada, confused, smiling the demure smile she knew that Silas favored. "Who are you talking about?"

"John Wilkes Booth," said Silas, replacing the book on the shelf amongst its fellows. "The man who killed Lincoln."

"I'm sorry?" said Ada, still smiling.

Silas raised an incredulous eyebrow. "Abraham Lincoln," he said. "The President of the United States"

"I thought," said Ada with a titter, "I thought that the president's name was Harrison."

With the heaviest sigh he ever did heave, Silas explained to her that Lincoln was the president when she was born and that he died several weeks later. She argued, again with that titter that she knew both annoyed and aroused him, that she should not be faulted for not remembering something that had happened when she was yet a mere babe.

"Aye," he said, "but you can be faulted for never learning it in all the years since. My God," he said, pushing his thinning hair back from his brow, "I knew you were born into the mud sill of society, but I had no idea how little—"

She set two fingers to his lips, shushing him. "Husband," she said. "I have news for you."

"What news?" he said, setting his hands upon her abdomen. "Is it the child?"

Ada peered deep into his eyes, searching there for the answer the dregs dared not give her, and then pulled away. She didn't know what to do. She should have told him weeks ago that the child was gone, that there might never have been a child in the first place, that the blood had, more likely than not, just come later than usual. A trick of the moon, that prankster. She didn't know what to do, so she stalled.

"Silas," she said, wrinkling her nose. "Silas, you reek. What have you been up to?"

Silas wrinkled his own nose, confused. "I reek?" he said.

"You do."

"I can't smell a thing."

Ada seized the opportunity to steer him further away from the subject of the child, to give herself some time to plan her next move. "Perhaps," she said, "you're coming down with a touch of something. For I smell it clear as—"

"I am not sick," he protested. "And I do not reek!"

Now she raised an eyebrow, albeit a less incredulous specimen than his.

Silas raised one arm and sniffed, then the other. Then he harrumphed. "I did," he admitted, "chance upon a gander pull on the way home." Now he nodded, removing his jacket. "That must be it. The stench of the ruffians must have clung to my coat."

Ada asked: "What's a gander pull?"

"You've never seen one?" he said.

She shook her head no.

"Perhaps you were born further from the mud sill than I suspected." He smiled and shook his head. Silas loved the chance to explain things. As chance would have it, Ada *had* laid eyes upon the spectacle in question more than once in her youth. But Silas didn't need to know that, at least not at this moment.

"They hang a goose," Silas told her, "upside down by its feet. Then they take turns riding by on horseback, trying to twist its head off."

It was quite a sight, she remembered. Her father, in fact, had been quite efficient at the avocation. Too good, she recalled. The other scoundrels in his circle always held him back until the end, so as not the spoil the sport.

"That sounds disgusting," she said, holding back a smile at the memory of her father on horseback. Ever dashing. Even in death.

In her moment of reverie, Silas caught sight of the box at last. "What's in the box?" he asked. "Ada, what is in that box?"

"Oh," she said. "That."

"Is that your news?" he asked, his dander up, his chest beginning to heave. "Do not continue to pile on the agony, woman. Is our child in that box? Is that your news? Have I lost another—"

The truth spilled from her then, as if he'd cut it out of her with the sharpness of his words.

"How long have you known?" he asked, stalking away from her, seething.

"I know I should have told you sooner," she said, "but I didn't know how."

"I should, by now," he said, "no longer be astounded by the the breadth and depth of things you don't know. Alas—"

"But I have taken steps," she told him, a little more desperation in her voice than she would have liked. "I know you don't always approve of my ways, but this will work. I know it. The leaves have told me so," she fibbed. She knew they would have told her eventually, so she did not think this an outright lie. Just a fib. A little one.

Silas turned to face her, his face flush, his skin redder and hotter than tarnation itself.

"The leaves?!" he shouted. "You entrust my legacy to leaves? I tore down my mother's house for you, you ungrateful strumpet. You said it was beset by evil spirits, and I built this sprawling, garish mess in its place—*for you*. When you said the spirits might linger here still, I bedded you in every one of these eleven rooms, searching for the purest of the lot. And now," he said, "now you tell me that *leaves* will help us to conceive a child?"

She breathed in deep and out slow. In deep and out slow. Then she nodded. "The leaves," she said, "and the contents of this box."

"What is inside this box," he asked, "that will assure our success?"

She smiled. "Open, it, husband, and see for yourself."

Ada watched, with fingertips clenched between her teeth, as Silas unwrapped her gift. As anxious as he might have been to see what was inside, he still untied the knot in the twine rather than snapping her neatly built bow in half. And he still untucked one corner of the wrapping at a time, instead of ripping the paper unceremoniously from the box. But then the moment of truth came and he could not hold himself back any longer. When at last the lid of the box presented itself to him, he threw it back and stared inside.

His face went white as he withdrew the weathered boot from its box and held it before him.

Ada reached into the box and plucked from its depths the scrap of yellowed newsprint she'd hoped he would find to help explain things. But he had no eye to spare to examine the paper; both were trained on the boot.

She read the clipping aloud to him. "Lost overboard," she began, "November 13th, from the schooner Minna of Harwich, Mr. Silas Silver, aged 28 years. He has a left a wife, three daughters, and a son. The man's foot, boot, and stocking, the latter marked SS (which drifted ashore early in December near P'town) belonged to Mr. S. His wife identified the mark on the stocking."

"Alas," Silas mumbled, still examining the boot, "poor Yorick."

"Who?" asked Ada.

"I knew him well," said Silas, a single tear rolling down his still blanched cheek. "If only," he mumbled. "If only."

"I thought your father's name was Silas," said Ada, holding the scrap of newspaper out for him to see. "That's what it says here in the clipping. That's what you've always told me. Who's Yorick?"

"Where did you find this?" asked Silas, finally looking at her again. He offered up the boot by way of explanation.

She told him how she'd found it beneath the floorboards of the kitchen, how it had called out to her. She asked, "Have you never seen it before?"

"I haven't," he said. "I never saw it."

"You knew nothing of this relic?" she said. "Nothing at all?"

"Oh, yes," he said. "I knew. My sisters told me of it. Many nights in my youth, in those years after I was deemed old enough to know how my father died, I could think of little else."

Silas rose and began to pace around the edges of the room, circling his wife. As he continued to speak, he kept a firm grip on the boot with one hand and stroked the books he passed with the other.

"I still remember the nightmare," he said, "how it haunted me. And most troubling was that it never ended the same way twice. Oh, if only there had been some sense of continuity, some sticky end I could have anticipated with dread each time, then it might have been easier to bear. But no. One night, it was the simple pain of seawater flooding my lungs; the next I might be swallowed whole by a great white whale; and the night after that I would walk the plank and plunge into the embrace of the shark below, feel my flesh torn asunder, watch my foot and my boot float off toward the shore, borne along on waves dyed red by my blood."

"Your blood yes," said Ada. "But your foot? Your boot?" She pointed. "That was your father's."

"Oh, of course," he said. "But it was a curse from my father—sire many children, as he had, or suffer the same death he was suffering then."

"Ah," she said, standing as he passed and taking hold of his arm to hold him steady. "But what if he never meant for it to be a curse?"

Silas shook her off and continued to brood. "It's all nonsense anyway," he said. "We speak of his legacy as if he were prepared to bequeath it. But he had no idea. His death was an accident. He thought he'd have years to pass on what he meant to pass on."

Ada scoffed and told him that was hopelessly naïve.

"Naïve?" he said. "How so? Explain that to me."

"He was a mariner, Silas. Certainly he knew the risks of his profession."

"Maybe he did, maybe he didn't," said Silas, ceasing his pacing at last. "But that is immaterial," he said as he collapsed into his chair. "What matters now is why you have brought this boot before me, why you have dug up old bones best left buried."

She knelt before him and set her hands upon his knees, rubbing as she told him that to leave things buried was to deny their power. When he asked her "what power?" she told him: "The power to conceive a child."

Silas laughed, as great a guffaw as she had ever heard from him. "Am I to bend you over my knee and fuck you with his boot? Am I to believe that his virility is so unmatched that my father might impregnate you from beyond that grave? That his seed might spring forth from the desiccated flesh of his big toe?"

Ada tore the boot from his grasp and shook it in his face. "Four children he sired. Four! The path he laid out for you is clear, but it is ground on which you fear to tread."

"What path, woman? You speak in riddles. You speak nonsense."

Ada shook her head. "You're afraid."

Silas wrestled the boot back from her and smacked her across the face with it. As Ada fell sideways to the floor, he rose to his full height above her. He seethed as he unbuckled his belt. "You think it is fear that has kept me from spreading my seed? Fear?!"

There came then a deafening crash of thunder. Both Silas and Ada looked around, confused, but Ada's eyes soon focused on the boot.

"The skies were clear," said Silas. "What mischief is this? Ada, what are you up to?"

Ada smiled as the weather provided the answer that the tea leaves had not. Silas grabbed at her necklace and pulled her toward him.

"Don't be angry," she said. "My love, I have done this for for the both of us. Don't you feel it?" She felt her body readying itself, hoped that his would follow suit. "It's been a long time."

"Feel what?"

"I have conjured him, Silas. I have summoned the one who can help you, who can help *us*."

Silas straddled her, her necklace still tight in his clenched fist. "Conjured?" he said. "Summoned? I don't need any help!"

He yanked her to her feet by the necklace then, spun her around, and bent her over the arm of his chair. It wasn't the way she had imagined it, but if this was the way the spirit was to take him—if this was the way he was meant to take her—then so be it. It would all be worth it in the end. She knew this to be true.

Thunder cracked again, shaking the very floorboards beneath their feet. And then, with a flash of lightning, all light was gone from the room. Rain began to pound down on the roof above and Silas seemed to have quit his business behind her. She could feel him stiff against her through the fabric of her bloomers, but her bloomers had yet to be torn asunder.

"Silas?" she said.

His hands squeezed her hips as he said, "Quiet, woman! Do you hear that?"

The front door creaked open, seemingly of its own accord. The roar of the maelstrom grew louder and louder. But through it all, if Ada listened hard enough, she could hear the squelching of footsteps making their way through the mud outside.

Silas let her go and pulled up his pants. She collected herself and straightened her skirts. But neither of them made for the door. Neither of them made to close it. It was if they both knew, and had silently agreed, that there was no point to deny what was coming for them now.

Presently, the feet they'd heard found the wood of the front steps. And then a figure began to ascend toward them, making its way toward the threshold.

It was ghastly, this apparition. Its hat was in tatters, its topcoat riddled with holes, and every inch of its body was draped in sea weed. Even the rusted musket it was using as crutch. Ada looked down the length of the figure and saw that, sure enough, one foot was missing.

"Who are you?" Silas said, bellowing to be heard as he drew his wife to him.

The figure made its way toward the discarded boot and plunged the stump of its severed leg into the boot's open maw. It tested the leg once, then twice, and when it was satisfied the mangled thing could take its weight, the figure cast aside its crutch, letting it thump to the floor.

"Who are you?" Silas screamed once more.

"Get off of her," said the figure, its voice raspy from disuse.

"Who are you?" said Silas.

"I said get off."

The figure waved a hand at Silas, and Ada watched in surprise as the gesture sent her husband hurtling away from her.

"Silas," she asked the figure, "is that you?"

"What are you on about?" asked her husband as he stood and brushed himself off. "I'm Silas."

Ada pointed toward the figure and smiled at her husband. "And so is he."

The ghost of her husband's father began to unbuckle his belt, and Ada saw clearly now what was meant to be. She bent at the waist to remove her underpants. Then she hiked up her skirts and sat herself upon the windowsill to wait.

"No," said her husband as the ghost made its way toward her. "No!" he said. "I can do this myself."

Husband grabbed ghost by the shoulder, but ghost was having none of it. With a flick of his wrist, the ghost slapped his son to the floor. Then he stepped on the fallen man with his mangled leg and pulled his bloodied foot from its boot, the ruined thing clinging to the rest of him by only the thinnest threads of muscle and sinew. The boot sat atop husband's chest as ghost turned back to Ada to finish his job. And husband lay supine on the floor, wrestling with the seemingly immovable horror that pinned him to the spot.

"Ada," shouted the husband. "Don't! I can do this."

"No, you can't!" said the ghost as he stepped out of his water-logged pants, as he set himself between Ada's thighs. "I never taught you, son. I didn't live long enough to show you how."

Ada gasped as the ghost found his way inside of her. She wrapped her arms around his soaking wet body and leaned her head back against the window.

"This," said the ghost to his son, "is how it's done. Watch," said the ghost, as he began to thrust. "Watch, and learn."

ॐ

WHEN IT WAS OVER, when she'd screamed the name her husband and the ghost shared, Ada made to squeeze her thighs around her lover, to hold him inside of her for a moment longer. But he was gone.

Her legs quivered as she stumbled toward Silas to remove the boot from his chest. She knelt by his side to do the deed and felt the faintest trickle of the ghost's seed dripping out of her. It felt like a betrayal. She prayed that was all that was wasted.

Then, as if in answer to her prayer, she felt a flutter inside her womb and she smiled. "And there it is," she told her husband, holding his hand to her belly. "An end to our suffering and the beginning of our new life. It is done, Silas. I feel our child already."

Silas recoiled from her and stalked away. "Not ours," he said.

"Yes," she protested, standing and reaching for him. "Ours. No one will know. No one *need* know. The line of Silas Silver will continue."

Silas shook his head and shook her off of him. "Do you want to know something?" he said. "It was never really about him."

Ada sighed. "Don't stew over this, Silas. This is a happy day, whatever the circumstances."

"I am not stewing," he told her. "I am telling you a story. You see, the nightmare, it was never as much about him as it was about *her*."

"Your mother?"

"No!" he shouted. "Why must my story always be the next chapter of theirs?"

Silas reached into his vest pocket and produced an old photo. Then he handed it to Ada. It was wet now, from where the water-logged boot had soaked the fabric clean through, and Silas seemed broken to see it so.

"Tamson O'Rourke," he said as Ada examined the picture of the pretty young thing. "Every dream and every nightmare begins with her."

"A romance of your youth?" said Ada.

"The romance of my life," said Silas. "I dreamt us a beach once, where we spoke the Bard's lines to one another while my foot was borne off on the waves." He laughed then, though it was mirthless. "That was the last time I dreamt of my father's godforsaken boot, the last time it haunted me. Soon I was off to war, and dreamt each night of real horrors: visions of musket fire piercing my arms, my chest, delusions of cannon balls taking my legs out from under me." He closed his eyes, collecting himself, then continued. "It was Tamson's face that came to me in those moments, not some vision of a boot, not the specter of my long dead father or the memory of my mother and her well-laid plans for me. And it is Tamson's face that has kept me from giving you, or any of the others, what my mother so desperately craved."

"My dear, sweet husband," said Ada, setting the picture down and taking hold of Silas' hands in her own. "I had no idea."

"You had no reason to know," he said, looking down, looking away from her.

"Why do you shun me?" she said, squeezing his hands. "What

I have done, I have done for us."

"And what I do," he said, prizing his hands from hers with a gentleness she was not expecting, "what I do now, I do for us as well."

"And what is that, my love? What will you do for us?"

"Not us," he told Ada, still looking away from her. "Not you and me," he told her. He nodded at the discarded photograph of his long, lost love. "*Us*."

And it was then that Silas looked at her. But Ada saw it in his eyes too late to put a stop to it, the look she had seen so often in her father's eyes when he was at last let loose upon a gander.

Her husband wrapped his hands around her throat and squeezed. She fought against him as he strangled her, but it was no use. As he pushed her toward the floor, she reached for the discarded boot, clawing at the floorboards to reach it, but it was just beyond her grasp.

"Who knows what wicked growth dwells inside of you now?" he spat. "It may be the spawn of the devil or a mere figment of my tortured imagination, but I will chance neither. If a father I am meant to be, a father I will be. But not this way. Not. This. Way."

Ada slapped at his arms one last time, but he was too much for her. He was too much for her, and she was too soon gone from this world.

PANTING FROM HIS EXERTIONS, Silas let the body slip to the floor. Then he slumped into his chair and plucked the boot from the outstretched hand of what had once been his wife.

He held it out before himself and sighed. "To be, or not to be," he recited from memory. Then he laughed. A short, pained laugh, but a laugh just the same. "Oh," he told the photograph of Tamson, "it is never a question, my love. At least not one we answer for ourselves."

🌿 3 🌿

ANIMALS

1880

As you holster the gun, you think about his apple pie, the spices he uses, that pinch of cardamom he insists makes all the difference. You think about the way he stuffs so much in there that the crust almost sags, but doesn't. You think about the time he cooked one in a Dutch oven, under the New Mexico sun, leaving it there all day while the two of you rode north to take down the stage coach out of Concord, New Hampshire. Then you think about how he took that heist too far, how he took things too far with the woman he dragged from the coach. But only after looking at you for approval. Which, without meaning to, you apparently gave.

He didn't think about you in that way, or so he told you; you were no ordinary woman and he could never think of you in no ordinary way. You were his partner, as quick on the draw as any dude he'd ever rode with. When he asked you where you learned, and you told him it was from your brother—back home in Massachusetts, after the war—he said he was glad some good come out of them Yankees winning; he was a Tennessee boy himself and would've been a Reb if only he'd been a little older, had a mother a little less like a hawk and more like a sparrow.

"And tragic," she says. "The girl died before the war was over. One of a thousand hurts my Silas has suffered."

"But now he has you," you say, squeezing her hands.

Maggie smiles at you and repeats your words. "Now, he has me."

"And what a balm you must be."

❧

THAT AFTERNOON, as you lunch with your cousin Hugo, you are stricken once again by the malady that has plagued you since your days in Dallas, since the day the horse threw you onto the tracks just outside the city limits. "Sarah?" he says, trying to shake you out of it. "Cousin, what ails you?"

But your lips cannot muster even so much as a whisper. You are rigid, your body unyielding. There is sweat dripping down your forehead, sweat which plasters a lock of graying hair across your eyes. And as your cousin dabs at your clammy skin with his too-fancy handkerchief, the monogram embroidered into the silk sending a shiver down your spine—as he pushes the hair out of your face for you, you wish you could tear the errant strands from your scalp. You feel like a weakling. You are one.

When it abates—the horror that has become mundane in these, your latter days—you apologize for not forewarning him. You give his hand a squeeze as you tell him that a life well-lived has its costs. And then you get back to your cucumber sandwiches.

"You're voracious," says Hugo, digging in himself now. "What shall we tell Silas if there's nothing left for him?"

You give him a smile, recalling a play you took in during your stint in Manhattan. "We will say," you tell Hugo, "that there were no cucumbers in the market this morning. Not even for ready money."

You could've looked away when he done what he done to that girl, but you didn't. And she didn't have to look at you, but she did. There were no tears on her face, only anger and a little bit of pain. She would've cursed you with her lips if he hadn't told her to shut up, if she didn't fear he'd make her. So, she cursed you with her eyes instead. And that there, you got to feeling, was worse, so much worse. You forgot words all the time—what your mother said when there was nothing to bury of your father but the boot that washed ashore, the pleas of your brother when you told him you were headed west—but a gaze burrowing its way into your soul (your mother's scorn, your brother's sadness); that, you never forgot.

As you watch your old partner's body drop to its knees, you try to memorize the lines on his face, the particulars of his surprise, the way the scar on his left cheek curled up into itself as his jaw fell. Had you really tracked him all this way, across canyon and prairie, river and mountain? Hadn't he told you why it was *that* coach that drove him too far, why the woman's answer to his question—"Where you from?"—had pushed him over the edge? He must have.

He did.

You watch to see if his soul will flee the collapsing husk, and, if so, where it will spill from. The bullet hole perhaps? Will it emerge, baptized in crimson, doomed to roam the wastelands of the world to come as a red ghost, the worst of its kind? Or is that some yarn your mother spun for you, your sisters, and your brother, after Daddy was gone, to keep you away from the sea, away from war, away from trouble in general?

"What have you done?" your partner's woman asks you.

You look around the street, careful to look only with your eyes and not with the rest of your body. You've been here before—not in Hinsdale, New Hampshire, of course, but in a situation where you expect to have guns drawn on you from all sides. But there is nothing, no one, just the empty mills, quiet on a Sunday afternoon. Just a crying woman and the body of her man, which now, finally, collapses into a heap.

From your coat, you withdraw the papers, your license to kill him. You give them to the woman.

"What's a bounty?" she asks.

"He did bad things," you say. "The government, they've been looking for him."

"So, why not send him to prison?" she says, cradling his head in her lap, his blood staining the dainty lace handkerchief she dabs at the bullet hole. "That's what you do, when someone's done something they shouldn't. Not this," she says, choking on tears and snot. "Not this."

⚜

YOU SPEND the afternoon fishing the Connecticut River, the body bagged up beside you. In the morning, you'll head south to Boston to collect your reward. But, for now, you're enjoying the moment of quiet you've earned. This was your last job, the one you promised yourself you'd do after you two split up under the New Mexico sunset, the evening after he went too far.

Even as you ate his pie, as you watched him divide up the afternoon's spoils, you knew you would leave. You had seen him do a lot of terrible things in your time together, had done a lot of terrible things alongside him, but those stolen moments with the woman from the stagecoach—that was too much. The pie was scrumptious, filling, the only food you would eat for three days, as you ran from him to California, across the desert, looking for some way to redeem yourself. As you swallowed that last bite, closing your eyes to focus on that pinch of cardamom that—he was right—made all the difference in the world, you knew you would run, but that you couldn't run forever, that some day you would have to make right what he done wrong, what you done wrong.

"I'm through," you told him, as you passed him the tin plate, which you'd licked clean.

"Through?" he said.

You nodded, extending your hand for your share of the afternoon's take.

"Why?" he said. "The woman?"

"My share," you said, gesturing for him to give it here.

"You jealous?" he said, with a laugh.

You stepped round the campfire and grabbed the bag he'd sorted your money into.

"That's it," he said, slapping his knee, falling backwards, laughing so loud the coyotes in the hills laughed right back.

You stuffed your prize into your saddle bag and made ready to mount your horse. But then, then he grabbed you. Gentle-like, but still a grab.

"You want to see what you're missing?" he said, a smirk across his lips. "I'd be happy to show you."

"I thought you didn't think of me that way," you said.

"I don't," he said, "but I understand a woman's got needs, just as sure as a man. And we have been out here a long time."

You pried his fingers loose and climbed atop your mount.

"I'll be here a few days," he said, sitting back by the fire, going back to his pie. "For when you change your mind."

❧

THE STORY he told was that, after Nashville fell, a detachment of Yanks from New Hampshire stumbled across his family's plantation—literally stumbled, drunk off of Tennessee mash—and decided to, as they put it, turn the tables: they raped the white women while they set the black ones free. Your partner, not yet a man, was held by an alternating pair of blue-coated devils, and made to watch while his mama was defiled by the third. He'd heard tell in his travels since, from Northerners themselves, that the men of New Hampshire were the hicks of the north, the lowest of their low, and that that kind of behavior was to be expected of their ilk.

❧

WHEN YOU FINALLY GET A BITE ON your line, the joy is short lived. Behind you, you hear her coming, twigs breaking beneath those dainty shoes of hers—everything about her so tiny, so precious. You smell her, too; it's a fancy perfume—probably mail-ordered from New York—with a hint of citrus to it. You dive behind the body at the tell-tale sound of a hammer being pulled back, and even though you know there's plenty of meat between the bullet and you now, your heart races just the same.

The first shot ends up God knows where—probably in the river. But the second, the second is true; it finds its mark. The body lurches against you from the impact. You're almost ready to shoot, almost have the gun cocked, when the third shot gets you, grazes your shoulder.

She's good, damned good. You thought she'd struggle, that she'd be all rage and no skill, that you'd get your moment and maybe a spare moment besides. But now, now you have no ideas. If you stand up, she's going to kill you.

"What right do you have?" she screams. "What right do you have to judge?"

"I've seen what he's done," you say, wondering if she's out, if you've miscounted, if she's buying time to reload.

"You think I haven't seen?" she spits back at you. "I've seen. I've felt his rage. But it ain't my place to decide his fate. That's God."

You hear a shell drop, bounce off the rocks. Then, you hear her scramble to pick it up. And now, knowing she's out, now you leap to your feet and you put one in each of her knee caps.

The blood stains the ivory of her petticoats as she holds tight to one knee and then the other, unable to decide which one hurts the most.

You kick the shotgun away, surprised that's what it was, trying to figure out where your counts came from, and then you kneel down. You press the muzzle of your piece to her temple. When she yelps for help, you put a finger to her lips to shush her. But when she tries to bite your digit off, you sock her in the jaw with your fist and back away.

Standing up now, you say, "My right is to treat animals like animals. That's what I done to him. That's what I'm going to do to you."

"I ain't no animal," she whimpers.

"You felt his rage and did nothing about it? Sounds like an animal to me."

She laughs. "What would you know about men and women, you horse-faced cow?"

"I know," you say, crouching down again, putting the gun to her head one last time, "that if you act like a bitch, wagging your tail until some mongrel comes around to do his business with you... if you act a bitch, you deserve to be put down like one."

You say that. Then, you shoot her.

Her body, with a few kicks from you, it tumbles into the river. The body in the bag, you hoist that up onto your old nag. "Let's go," you tell the horse, starting the walk to the south and east, the sun setting behind you. In the hills, there's howling. When it grows too close, you howl right back. And then, for a moment at least, it's quiet again.

❧ 4 ❧

THE PATIENCE FOR TAMING

1865

The Widow Silver's home was the last ramshackle cottage on the path that Patience strolled to the sea. As a girl, walking hand-in-hand with her father to this very beach on Sundays after church, she had wondered what grand views might be possible from the house's dilapidated dormers. But now, as she watched the youngest of her betrothed's sisters standing upon the lawn as still as a statue, eyes on the horizon, Patience saw the truth of it: to look upon the ocean was kind of torture for the women of this house. How many widows had been made by that water out there? How many beneath this one roof alone?

"You're lucky," Sarah told her, as they made ready the yard for that evening's reception, "that Silas fears the sea."

"I'm lucky," said Patience, "that my father owns every cranberry bog between here and Buzzard's Bay."

Sarah took hold of Patience by the wrists then, and looked her straight in the eye. "You are a fine woman," she said. "My brother is lucky to have you."

But that night, waiting beneath the covers of her marriage bed for her husband to return from his labors at the hearth below, she wondered if he'd have her before she fell to sleep. Her foot tapping against the mattress in rhythm with her impatient heart, she longed to be had, to be known.

Patience knew that he'd *known* at least one girl before her—she had caught them canoodling in a carriage abandoned by one of her father's bogs—but she tried her best not to dwell on their abominable ardor. The Kissing Cousins were what every person in the town had called them, mongers of fish and rumors alike, but Patience took Silas at his word that he had repented those sins. Even though she had seen the look in his eye as he marched down the steps of the town hall holding hands with that half-Irish whore, even though she had listened to them laugh as they tried to steal from one another the piece of paper that announced them as officially intended, Patience took the words of her husband as the Bible truth. She had to, didn't she? If she closed her eyes, she could see him kneeling in the cold mud outside Charleston, confessing to the chaplain as men moaned in pain around him, as men died in the days between battles. If only she would close her eyes.

But she didn't want to, not anymore. Instead, she reached for his nightstand and plucked from it the tome that he'd left there. In the candle light, as she read the spine, the deckled edges of the pages tickled her fingers. And though it should have made her smile that he had a taste for at least one fine thing in life—and it *would* make her father smile when she told him—Patience frowned. She leafed through the book until she found the scrap of leather he'd left to mark his place, then frown turned to scowl.

Book in hand, she stormed from the room and made for the stairs.

"My love?" called Silas from below, something clattering to the floor as he spoke, as Patience stomped down toward him.

She found him standing by the now roaring fire, a bottle of wine in hand.

"Where did you get that?" Patience asked.

"My cousin Hugo liberated it from the priest's pantry," he said. "I was a bit nervous before the ceremony."

Patience looked to the floor to keep from looking at him and saw there a wooden cup rolling across the hearth.

"I," he stuttered, "was a bit nervous just now, too."

"Nervous?" she said, as she watched the cup roll into the flames.

Silas stepped toward her then and set his hands upon her shoulders. "Can you not understand?" he said. "You are a beauty, my—"

"Don't patronize me," she said, shrugging him off as she clutched his book to her chest.

"Oh," said Silas, the cloying tone upon his gravelly voice like a derelict dressed for tea. "My love, I'm sorry to have tried your patience."

She growled at him and paid him for his pun with a sharp *thwack* of book on shoulder. And then another. And another. "I am no shrew to be tamed," she said as she shook the book at him, as he grabbed her by the wrists.

"Are you not?" he said, smirking at her, delight twisting upward the corners of his lips.

Patience thought of her father then, as she struggled to break free of her husband's grasp. She thought of her father putting her to bed when she was a girl, of what he told her as he pulled the nightgown down over her body, as she held her hair aside and waited for him to lace up the back. "What is wanted," he said, "must be taken."

And so she kicked the bottom of her bare foot at her husband's shin. And as he fell to his knees, hollering in pain, she swung his book at him one last time, driving it into the back of his head. Silas collapsed to the floor, a hand clutching at the spot where she'd hit him, and he whimpered. "Stop," he said. "For God's sake, stop."

But she did not, and she would not. No. Instead, Patience

straddled him, pushing him onto his back as she pushed his night shirt up and away from his loins.

"Patience," he said, as she tugged at him. "Patience, I am not ready."

"This part of you," she said, as she mounted him, "this part of you that is mine by law now, that is mine until death do we part—it begs to differ."

WHEN IT WAS OVER, she staggered to her feet and leaned against the fireplace, the heat a balm for the places that ached now. On the floor, Silas sat up and tugged at the hem of his shirt to cover himself. "The wait," he said, "would not have been much longer."

But Patience was not listening to him. She was staring at the book that lay discarded now upon the floor, its pages soaking up the spilt wine. "I saw her perform once," said Patience, absent-mindedly. "Your beloved."

"She was not my—"

"Your *beloved*," spat Patience. She balled up the hem of her gown to sponge from her loins the mess that Silas had left behind, then she continued. "During the war," she said, "Father took me to the city to see a show."

"Which play?" said Silas.

"That one," she said, nodding at the book. "This one," she said. "The one you're playing at now."

"I'm not playing—"

"And she was exquisite," said Patience. "Far too good to be begging on the Common with a soliloquy."

"What?" said Silas, crestfallen. "I thought you said—"

"Oh," said Patience, with a laugh, "we went to see a show, but she was no part of it. Oh, no, no, no. The footlights of Scollay Square were not calling for your lady fair. Nor for anyone of her ilk."

She watched with satisfaction as her husband ducked his head in shame. But when he told her that she was just as cruel as advertised, she scowled.

"As advertised by who?" she said, watching as he rose from the floor, as he rose to his full height.

"By you," he said, looking down on her now. "By your lack of a suitor, by that sneer you call a smile. And," he said, grabbing hold of her chin and yanking it upward, "by the size of the purse your father paid me to take your damaged goods off his hands."

Patience slapped his hand away. "Why, I never—"

"And he never!" said Silas, seething. "Or so I'm told. And if a man of his particular passions is never going to take what he—"

"What are you implying?" said Patience.

"Not implying," said Silas, shaking his head as he made his way toward the stairs. "Telling. I am telling you that you are as bound to me as I am bound to you. And if misery is the chain you wish to shackle us together, so be it. I am already familiar with that weight. I can bear it," he said, plucking his book from the puddle. "Can you?"

And with that, with those words and a smirk for good measure, he took his leave of her, leaving it to Patience to decide if she would be tamed, if she could be, if she should be, after all.

5

THE CHARITY OF RUIN

1870

Y ou stand betwixt your sisters as the rain falls, the branches of your family's ancient oak your only shelter from the storm. Racket still in hand, you stare at the shuttlecock laying discarded in the grass before you. You stare as hard as you can, glaring at it in the hopes that all your attention might be spent on the tiny, waterlogged thing, that ears might follow eyes, that you might hear nothing but the sound of the rain splattering against the birdie's feathers, against the leather and cork of its cap. But there is no escape from the prattling fools against whom your shoulders now press, no escape from the yarn they're spinning now that the game is over.

"And so," says Mary, the eldest, "into the wash basket he went."

Elizabeth, the middle child, chortles.

But you do not laugh. And when you do not laugh, you are nudged in the ribs for this slight against your sisters.

"Sarah," Mary says to you, wrapping her slender fingers around your gloved hand. "Have you heard a word we've said?"

"She's not listening," says Elizabeth, tut-tutting.

When you were out west, you shot people for less. But you

suppose you owe her at least one tut-tut for your willful disregard of her apparent wisdom.

"If you are to choose one suitor over another," says Mary.

"Then you must be prepared," says Elizabeth, finishing the thought, "to do terrible things to set right the mind of the also-ran."

"They are," says Mary, "both of them, enamored."

Elizabeth plucks the racket from your grasp and tosses it onto the grass. And now each of your sisters has one of your hands. For a blissful moment, you imagine them pulling in opposite directions. You see yourself suddenly as the sow your gang tied between its horses that one night in Arizona when it seemed the sun would never set. They had tortured the poor thing as they stole it from the delinquent's farm, as they dragged it past that man they'd beaten bloody and left under the hot sun, and you had been happy to see it put out of its misery. You had even tied one of its legs to your own mount to help speed the process, to end the suffering. And just as you helped to draw and quarter that poor beast, you hope to be halved now. For that is the only way to satisfy them both.

But they do not pull you apart. Instead, they wrap their arms around you and you find yourself sandwiched between two women for the first time since that brothel in Virginia City.

The experience is not nearly as pleasant.

Later, in bed, Charity laughs as you tell her all this. And you smile as the guffaw catches her off-guard, as she covers her mouth with her hands and looks wide-eyed toward the door.

"Are you afraid you'll wake Silas?" you ask her.

"Should I be?" she asks you. "He's been your brother far longer than he's been my husband."

You gather her face in your hands and bring her mouth to yours, intending to make the kiss a short one, the briefest of pecks. But your tongue and hers, they have minds of their own, and soon you are back beneath the bedclothes.

AT THE BREAKFAST table the next morning, sitting across from your brother, you stay silent on the matter of Charity's empty seat. Silas has been staring at it since the moment you set his bowl down before him, has been staring so long now that your bowl is empty, that your spoon's been set aside.

You watch the last bits of steam curl off his meal and into the air between you. You watch and wish there were something you could say to cure what ails him. But even an admission of guilt on your part, even the truth of why his wife came to his bed so late last night and has not yet risen today—even that would not lighten the burden he carries upon his shoulders. There is no sacrament save one that can undo the curse your mother visited upon him in her latter days. And it is only Charity who can give this blessing. But like Patience before her, she—or, rather, her body—has heretofore been disinclined to acquiesce.

You say, by way of a joke, "Perhaps the next time you marry, you should find yourself a woman of less virtue."

He quits his staring finally, but only to cast his troubled gaze on you.

"Patience," you explain. "And now Charity. Perhaps you should stay away from Hopes and Faiths the next time around."

You hope he'll at least give you a weak grin, but he can't even manage that. Instead, he ignores your play on words and says, "My marriage is a young thing. It may yet prove fruitful."

"It may yet," you tell him, standing as you collect your bowl and spoon. "And at least she's not a Prudence."

"Or a Chastity," he mumbles, finally beginning to eat.

You bend to kiss his forehead and acknowledge his attempt at levity, however half-hearted it might have been.

From the window above the kitchen sink, you watch the tide rolling out and think of the afternoon stroll that Charity has promised you. Arm in arm, you'll walk the length of the beach that stretches from your brother's front door to the mouth of Red River. Arm in arm, you'll search for a quiet spot among the dunes. And then, arm in arm, you'll plop your bottoms onto the sand, falling into each other as you laugh at your ruined dresses, as you laugh at the very notion of ruin itself.

"I am glad to have you here," your brother tells you as the legs of his chair scrape across the floor, as you hear him hoist himself up from his seat.

You offer him a smile from over your shoulder as you get back to the dishes.

"And I am sorry," he says, "that the lady of this house is so derelict in her duties."

"I don't mind," you tell him, already finished with the task, already drying your hands.

"I know you don't," he says, a hand on each of your shoulders now. "You are a good woman, Sarah. As good as Mother once was."

You shrug him off, unable to bear the reverence in his eyes. Just a handful of years ago, during her dying days, he was ready to put a pillow over the old woman's head. But now, it seems, he would build a pedestal for her if only he had some marble to spare.

You hang the dishrag in its place and stalk off toward the door. It is a good, long moment before he moves. You hope that he's caught a whiff of his own horse shit, though you don't hope too hard.

"She was a good woman," Silas is saying as he gives chase down the front steps. "A hard one, but good."

"This is the part," you say, wheeling around to face him again, "where you say 'given the circumstances,' right? Is that what's coming next?"

"Our father—" Silas begins, before you cut him off.

"Our father was not the only man overboard," you tell him. "A widow is nothing special by the sea!"

And though he disagrees, though you know that every brick of his being has been laid upon the foundation of your father's "distinct" demise, Silas says nothing. For he has seen the look in your eyes, a look he reveres, a fury that was your mother's bequest to you, to you alone amongst your sisters.

"The way he looked at me," you tell Charity later that day, as the two of you watch the Red River empty into the sea, "I swear he would've fucked me if—"

"If he weren't your brother?" she says, and you try to keep a straight face. What you were going to say is *if he weren't married now*. So it's probably a good thing she's interrupted you. You weren't sure before if Silas had told her about the two of you, but you are sure now.

"Maybe that wouldn't have made a difference," says Charity. "After all, his first love was his cousin, wasn't it?"

You glare at her, a look she knows is meant to end the conversation. But she doesn't stop.

"Circle the wagons all you want," she says, "but Silas' love for that girl will always be at the center of this."

You scoff. "Tamson O'Rourke has nothing do with why you can't carry a child."

And now it is Charity who glares.

"What?" you say, though you know what's coming.

"There is a curse upon that house," she says, pointing. "Everyone knows it, every person in this town, all of us except for you poor wretches born beneath its roof."

"If you knew it was cursed," you say to her, "then why marry into it?"

She laughs. "Why does any pirate—"

"You're a pirate now?"

"My people were," she says. "Robbed and whored their way around the Caribbean for decades."

"I didn't know," you say, though now you recall rumors, whispers. "So," you say, "why does any pirate—?"

"Plunder!" she says, finally finishing her thought. "Why does any pirate plunder?"

"I don't know," you say.

"Well," she says. "The money, for one. But beyond that, it's the challenge. The notion that whatever curse has been laid upon the hoard, you can beat it."

There is a tear in her eye as she says this, and something catching in her throat. Something like a sob. But she turns from you before you can be sure. And by the time you've circled round to see what's the matter, she has recomposed herself.

"It has been wonderful to have you here," she says, taking hold of your hands in her own. "But you mustn't stay."

"You don't think I—?"

She squeezes your hands to make you stop. "That house will make a spinster of you," she says. "If you let it."

"You would have me marry," you say, "when you could keep me all to yourself?"

She looks down, manages a weak smile.

"What kind of pirate are you?" you say, throwing her hands aside and stalking off.

❧

AN HOUR LATER, as you mount your horse in the sun's dying light, she has still not returned. You have told Silas to go after her, to fetch his wife, but he says he will wait and see you off. He holds open the gate in the fence your mother made him whitewash every Good Friday, and you smile at the bare wood you see between his fingers now. Whether by accident or intent, you are pleased to see that he has let some part of her go.

"Won't you stay?" he asks. "I'm sure that whatever—"

But you hush him with a raised hand before he can finish, and he gives you a resigned nod as you guide your horse from your mother's home for what you hope will be the last time.

On your way out of town, you pass the homes of your sisters: twin monstrosities sat beside each other on sloping lawns, bastards of brick and beam raised by their well-to-do husbands. No one is home at either place, so you leave notes on each doorstep for them and for their suitor of choice.

As soon as you've cleared the limits, you cut into the first piece of wild country you can find and you coax your steed into a gallop. The sun is stealing away from you. But you have a rope in your saddle bag, and a horse that'll run itself ragged if you only ask it to, so you're pretty sure you have a chance. You're pretty sure you can catch it if you keep trying.

6

THE BEST THING FOR BOTH
OF US

1895

Three years was the rumor. Three years of celibacy, one for each wife he'd lost. But when my sister turned up on the porch of the garish Victorian he'd built for his last bride—that half-Indian harlot—when my sister rapped her fist upon his door, he told her she was three days off. She had miscounted.

"I most certainly have not," she told him. "Silas Silver, I was here the day that your darling Ada passed to glory. I presented you with a stew fit for a king on this very veranda."

"And I did savor your mother's cooking, Miss Carson. I did indeed."

She did not appreciate the way he looked upon her as if she were still the dutiful child who'd held our mother's pot, but she could tell he wasn't finished. So, she stayed silent.

"But my vow," he said, "did not begin that day."

"Silas Silver," she said, "you make no sense whatsoever."

"I loved my Ada until the day they put her in the ground, Miss Carson. And that day," he said. "That day was the day my vow began."

"The day she was buried?" said my sister.

He nodded.

"I'm three days early?" she said.

"You are indeed," he said, though not unkindly.

She looked down then, could not help but notice how ridiculous her breasts looked, pushed up and out as they were by the contemptuous corset she'd had me pull her into that evening, that damnable thing that was suffocating her now.

"You have grown into a lovely young woman," he told her. "And I am not refusing your offer altogether," he said, lifting her chin so that he might look upon her face again.

"But I must wait," she said.

"As must I," he said, and then he stepped back into his house and closed the door.

THAT NIGHT, weeping into my shoulder, she lamented the fact that he'd made a fool of her. But when I told her, as I stroked her hair, that a fool made in the forest is no fool at all, she was not comforted. And perhaps that was because my metaphors have always been as half-made as my marriage beds, but I think it was truly because she didn't care if there was no one there to see her turned away. She knew what had happened. And so did Silas, that son of a bitch.

"Oh," I told her, "it doesn't do to disparage the dead."

She pulled away from me and raised an eyebrow as she sniffled.

"Oh, but that's right," I said. "You weren't yet born when old Widow Silver shuffled off this mortal coil. So, how could you know?"

"How could I know what?" asked my sister.

"That she was exactly as you described her."

My sister looked positively bewildered now. Both eyebrows were raised, her jaw was drooping, and her whole head was listing to one side. Confusion blew in across her face like a strong wind against her gentle sails.

"A bitch," I said, by way of clarification. "You called him a son of a bitch, and by God that's exactly what she was."

Her countenance unfrowned itself at this, and she broke into as boisterous a guffaw as ever I did hear from her.

It was a joyful noise and I smiled at myself for having brought it forth from her. But deep inside me, a message in a bottle tossed about on waves of my own making, a truth inside it that I knew would reach her eventually. I could only hope it would remain hidden from her until such time as I had reached the opposite shore. I shuddered to think of what manner of scream might rage forth from her pouty lips when that day came.

And when I shuddered, she found me a shawl and draped it over my cold shoulders. Then she kissed my cheek and bade me good night. She was off to bed to plot her next move, she said. Because, she assured me, there would be one. And then another. However many it took. Silas Silver, she promised me, would not have the last laugh here. Not by a long shot.

৩✲৩

ON THE SECOND NIGHT, she walked past his door with nary a knock upon it. Down the road she strolled, until she reached the beach at Red River, where she knew, from a lifetime spent watching him from our home on the hill across the water, that he took his evening constitutional.

Hiding behind a dune and casting ample glances over her shoulder throughout the endeavor, she stripped down to a bathing costume a Southern cousin had sent north to us after winning second place in a so-called "beauty" pageant. Then, her cheeks flush and the goose flesh on her arms and legs in fine form, she sauntered into the surf.

A chill shook her to her soul as the water wrapped round her ankles, but the sea air was bracing as she drew it into her lungs, so she threw caution to the wind and her body into the waves.

Gasping as she emerged, she caught sight of a scandalized Silas watching her. She caught her breath, offered him a smile, and then begged him to come hither and join her. His eyes followed a trickle of water she felt navigating its way from the hollow of her neck toward the more hallowed hollow below. His eyes on her bosom now, she asked him again to heed her call. And she swore she could see him take half an involuntary step toward her before he steadied his resolve and himself.

Not yet halfway through his walk, he was so flustered he could not manage a response. And so, he took his leave of her and made for the sanctuary of his home.

For a moment, she thought to cry again. She thought of the long walk through town to the closest bridge that would bring her home. She thought of eyes on her now-soaking body that she'd hoped would not look upon her again until she was his bride, or at least his betrothed. But then she took a deep breath and held back the maelstrom brewing behind her own eyes, and she remembered our father's words that no defeat is a true defeat without a white flag waved, that every battle, won or lost, is a victory until it is not.

What he meant by that, aside from a general note of encouragement, I can scarcely say. But it was all my sister needed in that moment. And all I've needed in moments of my own. So, I'm thankful for that, for that one bequest he saw fit to offer us before he was gone for good. Just as I was thankful that my sister came home that night without catching her death of cold, and with so much on her mind that she did not pause to ask me about the letters I'd strewn across our kitchen table in her absence. Thankful for the moment, but mindful—fearful, even—of the moment to come.

ON THE THIRD NIGHT, only one course of action remained, only one path to victory. And though I should have stopped her, though I should have laid myself bare before her—instead, I listened to her plan to lay herself bare before him. And when she was finished, when I had one final chance to dissuade the girl, to call her folly what it was, I simply laughed at her audacity and wished her well.

Whilst Silas took his walk that evening without issue, without encountering so much as a wayward crab or a scheming gull, my sister snuck into his house and deposited her naked body into his bed as a good faith payment on the debt she would owe to him if he rescued her from our broken home.

Beneath the covers, waiting for him, she explored the only collateral she had to offer, explored it as she often had in the years of waiting, and she made herself ready. Fingers found familiar places. And behind closed eyes, she saw clearly the imminence of her victory. When the door creaked open downstairs, she smiled the certain smile of a woman who knows she will not be refused. And she waited.

When he appeared at the door, he gave a little start, holding a hand to the flush chest she could see now through his unbuttoned shirt. But the shock was soon replaced with a smirk. He told her that she was nothing if not persistent.

"And will you reward me for that virtue?" she asked him.

"Miss Carson," he said, suddenly serious, "There is no reward for virtue in this world, certainly not in any prize I might offer."

My sister sat up then, let the sheets fall away from her bare chest, all modesty gone. "Then let me reward you," she said. "You have waited so long."

"And I will wait at least one night more," he said, handing her underclothes to her and averting his eyes.

"No," she said, throwing her brassiere at him, then the rest.

He turned to face her as she stomped toward him, laughing at her brashness as she fumbled with his belt, only taking hold of her wrists once she'd finally managed to unbuckle him.

"My vow," he said. "I have made a promise."

"To who?" she said as she wrenched herself free of him. And then, as she slapped one open palm against his chest and then the other, she said it again:

"To who?"

"I cannot say," he told her. "I am sworn to secrecy."

"Another promise," she said, shaking her head. And then, when he would say nothing more to her, she dressed and she left.

ᘓᘏᗷ

I CONFESS THAT, for a moment that night, I thought she had won him over. As I waited in our parlor, the clock chiming midnight, I fixed my eyes on the front gate and tried not to cry. I worried over the letters as a papist might worry over a set of rosary beads, folding and unfolding them without stopping to read even a word. I wondered suddenly if he had ever done the same. And I wondered if my words and the paper that had delivered them to him were but tinder now for the fireplace that sat at the foot of his bed. I wondered if he had even told my sister what my letters were before he burned them.

But then she came storming through the door, making her way for the stairs. She climbed and she climbed until I heard the faint echo of the door to the widow's walk slamming open above me.

I thought of going to her as I gathered up the letters and tucked them away inside our father's old chest once again. I thought about it, but didn't. And of all the regrets of my life, that one weighs heaviest upon these shoulders that have been slouched down by the worser angels of my nature. Because she was up there still as the sun rose over Nantucket Sound and Silas Silver came calling at our door. She was up there with tears in her eyes as she watched him pull a bouquet of spring flowers from behind his back, tears of joy that turned suddenly bitter as he called out my name instead of hers.

I opened the door just in time to see her body come crashing down upon the gate, to see her impaled by the pickets as the light of the morning sky left her eyes. That light, and every other.

❦

WE WAITED three months to marry, Silas and me. It seemed the right thing to do. Just as, I'm sure, waiting three nights for me to lay before him the way my sister had seemed the proper amount of time to wait before seeing my damaged goods for what they were.

He was reading when I came to him the next day to suggest a visit to the courthouse might be the best thing for both of us. Shakespeare, it was, as it so often was. *Henry VIII.*

He nodded when I was done talking, never once looking up from the page.

I'm told that Henry's fourth wife was the first to survive marriage to him. That I share this distinction with her, that and our name, is a small comfort. Something to laugh at when the demons come. And they do come, don't you worry. I know what I've done, what I damn near dared him to do, and I know what it cost.

7

THE WHORE OF HARWICH

1900

You sit at your brother's breakfast table for the first time in thirty summers and you listen to his latest wife spin the yarn of how they were woven together. It was his stories, she tells you as you sip the too-strong tea she has conjured for you. It was his tales of woe that won her weary heart.

You try not to wince at each bitter swallow that crosses your lips, and you try not to covet the sugar bowl she has kept from you by folding her arms in front of it, nor to covet the goodly bosom making itself known beneath her bodice as she leans toward you to whisper conspiratorially the tale that topped all the others.

"Sarah," she says to you, "do you know how many wives your brother has had?"

In your mind, you run through the names just to be sure you haven't forgotten one. Then you tell her, "You are the fifth."

She slaps the table and leans back, "Wrong!" she says. "I am the sixth."

You feel an eyebrow raising before you can stop yourself. "Who have I missed?" you say, and then you rattle them off, counting them on your fingers. "Patience, Charity, Ada, Anne, and now you."

"Ah," she says, a broad smile spreading across her face, "but there was someone else before us all."

And now you know exactly who she's speaking of, but you close your eyes in puzzlement just the same. For there was no wedding between The Kissing Cousins. Your mother had not allowed it. And what your mother did not allow, your brother did not allow himself.

"Unfurrow your brow," Maggie tells you, taking your hands into her own. "Unfurrow your brow, swear you'll take my confession to your grave, and I will lay bare the sweetest secret of your brother's saturnine soul."

You do as you are bid and open your eyes on the bright face of a young woman in the thralls of passion. Though you are quite certain of how the story ends, you cannot help but wonder how this tale of lost love and love lost has so enamored her.

"Boston at mid-winter," she says. "Can you picture it? The drifts high upon the Common, a blanket of snow curled around the gilded dome of the state house sitting high atop Beacon Hill. And at the foot of that gentle rise where sits the hub of the universe, down there in the shadows cast by revolutionaries and men of stature most high, there stands a simple church. Simple, but most grand in its lack of audacity. And in that church," she says, "in that church stands a soldier, on leave from a war between brothers."

In your mind's eye, you can see him in his uniform, both the boy who left and the man who returned. And you wonder which it is that stands there. You wonder whether he has slipped into his chrysalis yet, or whether that moment has yet to come. And then you wonder if perhaps this is the moment, if it was not the war at all that changed him.

"A friar stood with him as they waited on the bride."

"Was this a papist church?" you ask, confused.

She frowns. "Silas said it was a friar. Are there not protestant friars?"

Over her shoulder, in the next room, you see your brother's collection of Shakespeare and realization dawns on you just as plainly as the sun rising in the sky outside. "There may be," you tell her, patting her hand, not wanting to admit impediments to the marriage of their true minds. "Continue," you say.

"They stand there, the two men, their gaze locked upon the front doors of the place, and they wait. They wait, and they wait until finally she makes her entrance—the actress! Fresh from the footlights of Scollay Square, her makeup streaked, fat snowflakes in her tousled hair, she races down the aisle while she fishes through her purse. An apology on her lips, she hands the friar what he is owed and looks upon her beloved. 'I'm sorry,' she says as he takes her face in his hands and wipes away her tears with his thumbs. 'I'm sorry,' she says again and again until he silences her with his lips.

"The friar says, 'You're getting ahead of yourselves, aren't you?' But they're not listening. They have waited and waited for this moment. Back home, down here—down the Cape—their families would not have it. The town would not have it. But in Boston, costumed finally for roles they have cast themselves in, instead of the parts they have played heretofore, in Boston they are free.

"They have one night together," she says, "before his regiment expects him back. And they spend it in the room she rents next door to the theater. In the morning, they argue over the birdsong they hear as sunlight fights through storm clouds."

You can hear them in your head, debating over the nightingale and the lark, and you wonder which bits of this are true. Silas and Tamson had believed the Bard's adage that all the world was a stage, so perhaps they *had* ended their wedding night with those words. Or perhaps not. It made a good story, either way.

"Maggie," you tell her, "it is beautiful tale."

He raises an eyebrow. "Do I know that phrase from somewhere?"

"Doubtful," you tell him, knowing full-well that Hugo has not ventured forth from the comfortable confines of Cape Cod in at least a decade. "But," you say, "Silas might."

"Oh," he says, with a strained chuckle. "Is that right?"

You tell him you meant no offense, then you give his hand another squeeze. "It's Oscar Wilde," you say. "A play of his that was in and out of New York faster than—"

"Faster than Wilde was in and out of Bosie Douglas, I'll bet."

You cover your mouth with both hands despite yourself, shocked not by his impropriety so much as by his considerable knowledge of British scandal.

"Shame about Wilde," says Hugo, shaking his head. "Nothing inherently wrong with being sodomite, is there? I mean to say, why should we look upon the queer proclivities of men with any greater disdain than we do the sapphic yearnings of our young women? Is there any real difference," he asks, dabbing a napkin at the corners of his lips, "between diving for pearls and bobbing for apples?"

You blush despite yourself. There is a real difference, you suddenly realize, between the lewdness of a lord and the bawdiness of a brawler. The men you rode the west alongside, there was nothing they wouldn't say. But back east—back here—even amongst the mud sill of society, there had always been a sense of decorum. There were things one just did not say. So, when they were said, it made all the difference in the world.

You fold you cousin's handkerchief and make to return it to him, but he holds up a hand to dismiss the notion. "Keep it," he says. "It came to me on a breeze, a lost thing whipping along the beach."

"And you have no need of it?" you ask.

"No," he says, "but you might."

"I don't follow," you say.

"The initials," he says. "That cloth, if I were to wager, once belonged to Marcus Standish himself."

"And?" you say. "Am I to sell it back to him? Is the man truly vain enough that it might be worth trudging into town to return it?"

Hugo laughs, a deep guffaw drawn up from the bowels of his barreled chest. "If I were to guess, Mister Standish has given so many of those away over these many years that there are naught but a handful of homes in all Harwich where one could not be found."

"Do you mean to suggest," you say, stifling a laugh of your own, "that the most infamous whoremonger in the county... What in tarnation would that man want with an old maid like me?"

"Were you not an adventuress in your day?" he says.

You throw the handkerchief at him, but he is quick, as quick as you used to be, and he catches it before it smacks him in the face.

"What would he want?" says Hugo as he folds the handker-chief once more. "This house, perhaps? This perfect perch at the edge of the deep green sea? You know that I've long coveted it, that it would belong to me and my sons if only your stubborn brother would admit defeat and accept the fruitlessness of his loins as the rest of us have."

"Well," you say, "I am fruitless now too, my branch as barren as Silas'."

"True," says Hugo, pushing the handkerchief back to you. "True. But permit me this: why have you returned here, at the end of your long life, if not to reconcile with your brother? And what better tool might you find to set at ease the mind of a man who still labors under the delusion that one of his wives favored you more than him? Show him this trinket, this token. You need say nothing more. He'll write the rest of the story in his head for you."

You look into Hugo's eyes and see that he is telling the truth, that your brother has indeed spent these many years suspecting you of what you long suspected he might suspect. You look into his eyes and you take the handkerchief and you thank him. Then he rises, kisses your forehead, and takes his leave of you.

WHEN YOUR BROTHER returns and asks for a sandwich and a cup of tea, you pick up the empty plate in horror and feed him the line. Without missing a beat, he waves a hand dismissively and tells you that it really makes no matter. "I had some crumpets with Lady Harbury," he says, "who seems to be living entirely for pleasure now."

You fall into each other, laughing. Laughing as you haven't done since your mother, in her grief, made you his nursemaid all those years ago. With your father dead and gone, your sisters had to be married off. And quick. But you, you she could spare. And so, you and Silas have always shared a great many things. Your bed, yes, once upon a time. And the love of your cousin Tamson. But before all that there were the blocks your father had carved on his shore leaves, the stories you read from your grandfather's dusty old tomes, the hand puppets you sewed when you and Silas and Tamson began to perform the Bard together.

"That was a dreadful play," he says. "Wasn't it?"

"I enjoyed it," you say. "For what it was."

"But what was it?" he says, smirking at you.

He collects the plates and takes them to the sink. As you watch him, you recall that morning, years ago, when you played out this same scene. It seems like only yesterday, you tell him, the day you left.

"Only you were the one cleaning the dishes," he says. "And the one sleeping with my wife."

You cannot see his face as he says this. You cannot read the feelings in his monotone. Across your forehead, you feel a sheet of sweat descending from your hairline toward your brow. And as you move to wipe it with your handkerchief, you struggle for some offhand remark to set his mind at ease.

"If one shares a bed with her friend," you say, stuttering a little as you search your mind for the line, "not meaning any harm..."

He shakes his head but does not look at you. "In bed and not mean harm?" he says, his voice still even and unperturbed, the pace of his words almost leisurely. "It is hypocrisy against the devil. They that mean virtuously, and yet do so, the devil their virtue tempts, and they tempt heaven."

"They do nothing," you spit out, all of it coming back to you. "'Tis a venial slip. But if I give my wife," you say, holding the object toward him before you realize what it is, what it really is. The embroidered initials lay beneath your thumb: an M and an S. But they belong not to Marcus Standish, you realize, but to Margaret Silver. Damn, Hugo. Damn him all to hell.

"A handkerchief," says Silas as he turns to face you again, only the hint of a frown upon his face.

You mean to hide the thing away, to tuck it away in your sleeve or into a pocket. You have time before he sees. But your hand will not move. Your arm will not. You are seized by your demons as his gaze moves from your face to your hand, as his countenance is overcome by shock and then grief. And then anger.

He tears the handkerchief from your hand, paying no mind to the state of you. "What is this?" he says. "Sister, do you mock me?"

You watch him as he stalks across the room, pacing the length of it while he stares at the blasted slip of fabric he clutches between his white-knuckled hands. And you want to tell him the truth of it, but your lips are just as much your enemy now as any other muscle in your body. Just as much your enemy as time.

Time, which runs out as the sixth of your sisters-in-law opens the front door and steps inside.

"Silas?" she says, setting a hand upon his shoulder. "What's the matter?"

He shrugs her off and wheels on her, shaking the handkerchief in her face. "You gave this to my sister?" he hisses.

"No," she says. "I lost it. You know that. I lost it on the beach, during a walk."

"A walk?" he says, snorting back a laugh. "You wouldn't be the first wife to take a walk with her."

"Ask her yourself," says Maggie, pointing at you. But then she sees what's become of you and races to your side. "Silas," she says, holding your wrist in one hand whilst she cradles your head in the other. "She's had another of them."

"Another of what?" he says, still seething. "Care you more for her than me? Whose woman are you? I say again: whose woman are you?"

"Yours," she tells him, shaking you, trying to bring you out of it.

"Lies!" he says. "Six of you, I have had now. And none have been true. Not a one. You have lain with her!"

"She will not say so," says Maggie. "She will not!"

"No," he says, stomping toward her and taking hold of her shoulders. "Her mouth is stopped. As yours, strumpet, must now be."

When he pulls her from you, you topple to the floor. And it is only then that you begin to feel a tingling in your toes and in your fingers. It is only as you watch him straddle her and wrap his hands around her throat that you feel the spell breaking.

"I... am... your... wife," she struggles to say.

"My wife?" he says, squeezing harder now. "What wife? I have no wife!"

"Silas," you rasp, crawling toward him. "Silas!"

He stops and lets her go, staring at you with his mouth agape and his eyes wet with tears. A boy stares out at you from behind the weary eyes of this aging man, a boy who knows he's about to be scolded, who knows he deserves whatever is coming to him.

"She spoke true," you tell him, pushing him aside as you listen for her breath, as you feel for her pulse. "We were deceived," you tell him. "The both of us."

"By who?" he says.

You say nothing for a moment, holding a finger to your lips to shush him as you lower your ear to his wife's face. It takes a moment more before you feel a shallow breath against your neck, as shallow as you've ever felt. "She lives," you say.

He closes his eyes, mumbles, "Who? Who, Sarah? Who?"

"Hugo," you say. "Our cousin has undone us." But then, then you rise to your feet, steadying yourself on the chair that still stands upright. You rise, take a deep breath, and look down at your brother as you draw your pistol from the holster at your hip. "Our cousin has undone us, but now I'm going to undo him."

And before Silas can say anything more, you are out the door and into the night.

YOU FIND Hugo on the beach, sitting amongst the dunes, cradling a crab's shell in his hands. You see him flinch as another shell crunches beneath your boot. But he does not stand, not yet.

"She lives," you tell him.

"Ah," he says. "My provocation was not potent enough."

You cock the gun as you circle to the front of him. Then you stare down the barrel at his unrepentant face. And still he does not move. "He tried to choke the life from her," you tell him. "But she lives."

"Ah," he says, "but what kind of life?"

You fire a single shot into his kneecap and watch as he collapses to the side, clutching at the wound as he howls in pain.

"I bleed, m'am," is all he can muster. That, and then: "I bleed, but I am not killed."

"I am not sorry," you say, crouching and pushing the hot barrel into the soft flesh of his cheek. "'Tis happiness to die," you say. "To meet your end feeling righteous and true. May you live forever, you bastard, crippled until the end of the world by the weight of your failure. Bathed in the stink of it."

He laughs at you as you walk away. Laughs and laughs and laughs. "Your words are hollow, cousin," is what he cries out to you. "We both know the truth of it! We both know the truth."

❧

MAGGIE DOES NOT WAKE. Not the next day, nor the one after that. When she does open her eyes, her stare is blank, her gaze empty. Her lips part when you press a spoon of steaming broth to them. Her throat and her stomach fulfill their roles. Her body plays its part. But her mind, it is far afield.

Silas paces the length of the house, mumbling curses at himself, at your mother, at what is left of his wife, sparing no one but you. He cannot bear to look you in the eye, though. He watches with sidelong glances as you do the job that he knows is meant for him. When you change Maggie's linens, when you wash her pallid skin—these are the only moments that still him. Once you've left the bed, once he sees you standing over the sink to ring out the washcloth over that basin, then he is right back to wearing a hole in the rug.

Years pass and you stay in one place for the first time since you were a girl. You thank heaven every day that your body does not seize you. You spend many a night sitting in bed with the barrel of your gun pressed to your chin, wondering if you should rid your brother of yourself before you become a burden too.

A decade passes before Maggie does. At the services, the townsfolk wrap their condolences in ribbons of praise, clutching your hand or kissing you on the cheek as they yammer on about how virtuous it was of you to stay and lend your support to your brother in his time of need. You smile and nod, smile and nod, staring longingly out the window at the horse you've hitched alongside the new-fangled motorcars parked out front. You know your hips wouldn't like it if you made for the door right now and leapt into that saddle. You know the cries of protest your weary husk of a body would let fly. But it doesn't hurt to *imagine* your escape, to maybe even plan a little of it. After all, you never would have notched so many miles on your belt if you hadn't spent at least a portion of each moment looking for a way to survive to the next.

When the bodies are gone from your brother's parlor, and the body too, you sit with Silas in silence and listen to the waves crashing against the shore outside his window.

"Should I try again?" he asks, after a good long while.

"You're nearly seventy years old," you remind him.

"It's what Mother would have wanted," he says.

And since you can't find fault with that calculation, you say nothing.

"Mary has had children," he says.

"And grandchildren," you add.

"Elizabeth, too," he says.

You turn to him, offer him a kindly smile. "Most would say that's enough. Most would understand that, though the name Silver dies with you, our blood still walks this earth."

He looks to the floor, as if he's still the boy you once raised, as if he might find a lost marble there. Or something more precious.

"But Mother wasn't most," you say, giving voice to that which he seems determined not to speak.

He looks at you with glassy eyes, the lids beneath them puffy with a watery weight he cannot hold back much longer.

"I would lift the burden from your shoulders," you say, "if only you would let me, if only my words were absolution enough."

"Nine Silases have lived here," he says, the tears rolling down his ragged cheeks now. "Nine Silases, at the edge of the ocean. And if I fail, I fail not only our mother, not only our father—"

You come to your feet and it knocks the wind out of his sails, shutting him up. "Nine Silases," you say. "Yes, nine Silases. But how many wives? How many women have been used up beneath this roof? How many by you alone? Six, Silas! Six! Don't you think God might be trying to tell you something? A farmer who sows his seed across six fields without a crop to show for himself—he can blame the soil all he wants, but any man with any sense..."

He comes to his feet now, too. "You go too far," he says through gritted teeth.

"I will go as far as I need to," you tell him. "I will..." you begin to say, but then you feel it, your body turning against you. For the first time in years. You close your eyes and you ball up your fists until you feel your fingernails piercing flesh.

"Sarah?" you hear your brother saying as the terror abates. "Sarah?" he says, taking hold of your shoulders. "You should sit."

You open your eyes and you look at him. You want to shrug him off, but this is the perfect opportunity to finish it. So you stare into him, into the deepest part of him you can find, and you say, "Will you stop?"

And he answers you not with words, but with a blink of those eyes that you cannot stand to look at any longer. So *now* you shrug him off.

And now you are out the door. Now you are untying the horse. Now you are stepping into the stirrups and not hearing a word he says in protest, not hearing your body as it tells you 'no' too.

"Sister," he says, clutching at your pant leg. "Don't go. Don't leave me."

You look to the late afternoon sky and see the moon of the evening beginning to rise. Once upon a time you rode from this place in pursuit of the sun. But now, now it's time to outrun what's coming for *you*. You look down at your brother, the fool, and you know he will only hinder you. He will only encumber you, as he does everyone he latches onto. So you shake him off one last time and you ride. You ride like there's no tomorrow.

Because now—the stench of Maggie's body still fresh in your nose, the revolt of your body still fresh in your bones—now you know for sure that there might not be.

❧ 8 ❧

THE CRONE ON THE COMMON

1915

The crone fled across the Common, and Annie followed. It was a struggle for her, with a belly fit to burst any day now. Nevertheless, she persisted. She might be nine months along, but Annie felt confident she would overtake the old woman in time. She'd been pregnant more often than not in the years since she first set her cap for a man, and she'd long since stopped her condition from stopping her.

The chase wound up the slope of Beacon Hill and past the gilded dome of the State House, then down the other side and through the streets and alleys of the West End. By the time they reached the river, Annie was all of a dither. The crone was making for a bar of some sort, a hive of scum and villainy if ever Annie had seen one—and she had seen more than her share in her days down the Cape. If she lost the crone there, amidst that crowd, all might be lost.

So she shouted at the top of her lungs to "Stop that vagrant," waving her arms to draw the attention of the patrons milling about the stoop. "Stop her! She's stolen my purse."

But they did nothing. Some of them cast a glance at the crone, yes—out of sheer morbid curiosity, Annie supposed—but not one lifted a finger to aid Annie's cause.

The truth was that the crone had stolen nothing from Annie, nothing save an overlong glance from across the way. But that look, the look in the old woman's eyes as she leered at Annie from the other side of the enormous fountain—there was something there that Annie had never seen before. It was a fierce look, yes, but that ferocity was tinged by an intense affection—and maybe, if Annie was right, even a sense of pride. It was as if the crone knew Annie in some way. But how?

Before she'd had a chance to ask, the old woman had run.

And now, making her way through the huddled mass of ne'er-do-wells ogling her as she passed, each of them focused on some other fine thing she carried on her person, Annie had indeed lost her quarry. She stood on tiptoe to peer over the heads of the throng, once and then again. But there was nothing doing. The crone was gone.

"You're after the old woman?" asked someone from behind her.

It was a hooded figure, one of six crowded around a small table. They looked like something straight out of the book of fairy tales she read each night to her precious Elijah—the first of her children not born a bastard, the first she'd been allowed to keep. They were a coven of witches, perhaps. Or perhaps a secret guild of huntsmen come to clear the king's woods after the death of his daughter. But there had been few witches in these parts since the people of Salem had taken to burning them alive, and there were no woods in Boston to speak of, at least not anymore. No, these traveling cloaks were as anachronistic an affectation as she had ever seen, and they were so tightly pulled around the figures that Annie could not make out any other detail. She wondered for a moment if they might not be characters from a fairy tale at all, if they mightn't be from Mister Wells' novel instead. Might their time machine be tucked into an alleyway out back? It was an enticing thought, a thread she might follow at any other time, but she was burdened with glorious purpose here and could not afford further digression.

"Yes," she told the strangers. "Did she see which way she went?"

One of them pointed a gloved hand at a door to the right of the bar, near the very back of the place. "You best hurry," they said.

And so she did, turning her belly this way and that to avoid elbows or worse, sweating so much it was as if tarnation itself were steaming up from between the floorboards. The door was a relief once she made it there, the draft that whipped across the threshold and between her jellied legs so refreshing that Annie might have stopped to rest her head against the jamb if not for the urgency of her undertaking.

Instead, she threw the thing open and stormed out into an alley way that was lit by an eerie orange glow. Annie searched for its source and was startled to find that the effulgence emanated from a what looked to be a tear in the very air. Or, now that she squinted at it, less a tear than the parting of two great curtains. Presently the light went out altogether. And then, from the darkness, Annie finally heard her quarry speak.

"Oh," said the crone. "Oh shit."

Annie doubled over, panting, clutching at a stitch on one side and the raging kicks of her baby on the other. "Who," she began, in between harried breaths, "are you? And what," she asked, pointing at the spot where the glow had been, "was that?"

"You don't want to ask me these questions," said the crone. "Annie, trust me: you really don't."

Annie stood bolt upright at the shock of hearing the stranger speak her name. Her jaw went slack and her voice deserted her.

"We can change things," said the crone. "I've done it before."

"Change what?" said Annie, raising an eyebrow in confusion. "Done what?"

"I..." the crone stuttered. "I've... I have visions sometimes. Visions of terrible things. And if I'm careful, I can stop them."

Annie watched the crone carefully. She was hiding something. The way she paused between words—it was like she was making this up on the spot, or at least part of it. But Annie could swear there was a sliver of truth in there somewhere as well, some small morsel. So, once again, she persisted.

"How do you know me?" asked Annie.

"You don't want to ask me that," said the crone. "You want to stop asking me questions altogether. That's the only way this will work."

Annie scoffed. "You don't know me at all," she said. "I'm the most quizzical person you'll ever meet." She puffed up her chest with pride. "Quizzical to a fault, according to my dear Silas."

The crone sighed and shook her head, then cast her gaze down at the ground.

"I'm sorry I exasperate you so," said Annie. "But I will have my answers."

"Quizzical to a fault," repeated the crone. "Did he really say that?"

"Yes, indeed," said Annie. "He's a man of a certain age, my Silas, and he cannot be—"

"He's a curmudgeon, you mean to say."

Annie looked down her nose at the stooped old woman and shook her head. "Each man on God's green earth is born with certain ration of patience. My Silas can't be faulted for having spent his long before he met me."

"Sure he can," said the crone, a smirk playing across her lips. "And he never had much patience to begin with, to tell you the truth."

"You knew my Silas?"

The crone laughed, then nodded. "You might say I was the first to *know* him."

"Who are you?" asked Annie.

The question sobered the crone straight away. She blanched, her pale, wrinkled flesh drained of what little color it had left. Under other circumstances, this transformation might have been enough to make Annie give up and give in. But the crone was spry for her age—their chase had proven that. She could take a bit more heat before Annie let her out of the kitchen.

"Who are you?" Annie asked again.

"There are too many answers to that question," said the crone.

Annie stepped forward and took hold of the lapels of the crone's moth-eaten topcoat. "Enough riddles!" she said. "Answer me."

The crone lay her hands upon Annie's belly then and began to cry, and Annie wasn't sure whether it was the touch or the tears that made her recoil so quickly and with such force. Both women stumbled backward away from each other, nearly falling to the ground before righting themselves.

"Annie," said the crone, through sobs that threatened to choke the voice right out of her, "this is it. This is your last chance. I've already said too much. And I am begging you: please don't make me say more."

Annie set her own hands upon her belly then, searching for movement, frightened. It had been the slightest of touches, the gentlest, but still she feared that this strange woman might have done something to her baby or might have meant to. After all: she'd seen the woman stitch together a tear in the air with nary a word or a gesture. Who knew what conjurations she was capable of? One of Silas' wives had been an enchantress of some sort, and she'd tried to snuff the life right out of him. Who was to say that the forces of evil had ceased their machinations against his family that day?

"Turn around," said the crone, wiping the tears away with her tattered sleeves, trying desperately to collect herself. "Turn around and go home, Annie. I am begging you."

But Annie stood her ground and asked one last time, "Who are you?"

The crone sighed. Then she began, saying: "I've had many names."

"No more riddles!" spat Annie, tired of the tricks, sick of the stalling.

"My name is Emily Henderson," said the crone. "Or, well, that's what it's been since I married Ernest some years ago. Before that, I was Emily Gold. But of course that was to keep my parents from finding me, or my husband's. It should have been Emily Silver, really."

"Silver?" said Annie. "But that's my—"

"Silas and I—for a moment, we thought that me using my middle name would be enough. But in the end, we decided it was too risky."

Annie's heart was all aflutter and she pressed a clammy hand to her chest to help steady the panicked organ. Was she hearing what she thought she was hearing? Could this be—? But she was dead, wasn't she? That's what her dear Silas had told her, that this woman had died during the war. Long, long ago. "Your husband's name was Silas, too?" she stuttered. "Si—Silas Silver?"

The crone cackled. "Not 'too,' dear girl. My Silas is your Silas now."

And with that, Annie swooned as she had never swooned before.

৩ৠ৩

WHEN SHE CAME to her senses, she was supine on the cold concrete of the alley floor. Above her, the first stars were peeking through the veil of dusk. And she would have lain there for a good while longer, her purpose here forgotten, if the crone hadn't stooped into view to adjust the traveling cloak that she'd taken off of herself and repurposed as a blanket for Annie.

"Oh," said the crone. "You're awake."

"How long was I–?"

The crone smiled. She wasn't missing nearly as many teeth as Annie had suspected she might be. "Long enough," said the crone, "to give an old woman palpitations."

Annie studied the crone's face as the old woman dabbed a damp cloth across her forehead. And she saw, for the first time since the fountain, that glint of affection she'd been searching for an answer for.

"Have you read any of Mister Baum's Oz books?" asked the crone.

Annie nodded. Gently, of course, for her head felt like it had been torn apart by a cyclone straight out of those novels.

"I imagine you feel quite like Dorothy," said the crone. "I only hope you don't think me the wicked witch."

The conversation was coming back to her now, the words that had swept Annie off her feet. It was said—never by Silas himself, for he was too good a man to compare any woman to another— that Annie was the spitting image of his first love, that that was why he was so taken with her. So Annie searched the crone's face for the resemblance, trying to imagine away the wrinkles and pockmarks and sagging skin and to see the Tamson O'Rourke that she'd heard so much about.

Tamson, she thought. The first wife's name was Tamson, not Emily.

"What?" said the crone, her gray eyebrows raised, her face screwed up as she tried, presumably, to tease out why Annie's own countenance had just gone sour.

"His first wife was Tamson," said Annie. "Tamson, not Emily."

"I told you," said the crone, wiping the cloth across Annie's brow once more, "we used my middle name to hide me from my parents. From Silas' parents, too. I haven't gone by the name Tamson since all before you were born."

"But," said Annie, "you died during the war. That's what Silas told me."

A painful smile played across the crone's thin lips. "Oh, I died a little," she said, "every time I thought of my love bleeding out on some battlefield. But I'm not dead, not yet."

"Then why would Silas—?"

The crone held a finger to Annie's lips and begged the girl's patience while she explained. Then she spun a yarn for Annie that was so colorful—and preposterous—that neither Mister Baum nor Mister Wells, for all their skill, for all their notoriety, could have pressed the public to believe it possible.

"I don't believe a word of that," said Annie.

"Do you think I could invent it?" asked the crone.

"Tamson O'Rourke was as much a student of Shakespeare as my dear Silas," said Annie. "If you are her—and I still have my doubts—then I'm sure you could invent just about any story you wanted. But you will not pull the wool over my eyes, ma'am. No, you will not."

The crone shook her head. "All you need believe is the bit about my abduction—that I came to this place in a moment of weakness and that I was stolen away from my Silas and from my dear..."

Annie stared at the crone as she trailed off, as she held a hand to her mouth, rolled her eyes in disgust with someone—with herself, Annie guessed—and sighed.

"Your dear who?" asked Annie. "There was someone else as dear to you as our dear Silas?"

The crone held a cold hand to one side of Annie's face, thumb stroking cheek. The other hand played with Annie's hair as the crone leaned in close and spoke. "I've said too much, Annie. But we can still stop this. Let me walk away, and we can—"

"Let you walk away?" said Annie, shrugging off the crone's hands and sitting up at last. "I've fainted in an alley way, with a baby fit to burst my belly at any moment, and you want to walk away?"

The crone stood and hurried back toward the spot where Annie had seen her tear the air in twain. Then the crone began to wave her hands about that spot again, as if searching for something. No, not searching. Conjuring!

"Answer me!" Annie shouted, trying to stand and then thinking better of it.

The crone found the edge of something there in the air, her fingers disappearing for a moment, and then she prized apart the curtains that Annie had glimpsed before. Behind the curtains, the sun was rising. It was the sun back there, Annie realized. But how? How?

"Who was as dear to you as Silas?" asked Annie.

The crone's head fell forward, pointed chin pressed against heaving chest. Then she let the curtains of darkness fall back into place, the orange light behind them blinking out of existence one last time.

"Who?" Annie asked.

The crone faced Annie with tears in her eyes. "My daughter," she said.

The words would not sink in, as hard as Annie tried to make them. Her Silas, who had married again and again in his efforts to start the family he had long dreamed of—trying, yet never succeeding until Annie had given him their Elijah—her Silas had another child, a child he'd never known?

"I left her that night," said the crone, "in the ramshackle room that we called home. I'd been out of work for months, since before the birth, since the moment I'd begun to show really. We'd been living off the kindness of friends, performers I'd worked with at the theaters around town in the months after Silas' departure. But I was tired of their charity, felt unworthy of it, so I took this body of mine that I'd spent weeks recovering, and I took it to a place where it might be of some profitable use to my baby and me. I thought I'd be back before she woke," said the crone. "But I wasn't."

"And what happened to her?" asked Annie.

"An orphanage," said the crone, still crying. But when Annie began to tear up herself, the crone sniffled back the last of her tears, straightened herself up, and added, "But not for long, dear. An Irish couple took her in, got her out of this city of misfortune and brought her with them down the Cape."

"And how do you know this?" asked Annie. "Did you come back for her?"

"I couldn't. But I've watched her," said the crone. "From afar. Watched as she grew and prospered, married herself a fine man, had herself many children, and even took in a few who weren't her own."

"Other orphans?" said Annie.

"Orphans?" said the crone. "No. Bastards," she said.

Annie smiled, thinking of her own mother's charity. The crone's daughter sounded so much like Annie's mother as to be laughable. It was only when her mother's hair began to grow more silver than a storm cloud, when she could no longer take credit for the children that Annie continued to deliver unto their doorstep, that Annie's parents had sought a husband for her.

"Sound like anyone you know?" asked the crone.

"As a matter of fact," Annie began, but then she stopped, and she felt her stomach churn as these words—as *all* the old woman's words—finally sank in. "What are you saying?" asked Annie.

"You know what I'm saying," said the crone, ducking her head away from Annie once more.

"But," said Annie. "If you're my mother's..."

"Then Silas is your mother's..."

"And," said Annie, her stomach now thrashing like the seas that stole her dear husband's father from him so long ago, "that makes Silas my... my..."

The crone ran to Annie then, seeing the color drain from her face. "Yes," she said, "but they are all just words, Annie. He is your husband. That is all that matters."

Annie fell backwards, her head bouncing off the alley floor. But her body would not grant her sleep this time. *No rest for the wicked*, Annie thought. And that's most certainly what she was. Wicked. *Wicked, wicked, wicked.* "Not just husband," she stuttered. "Also... also..."

And it was then that her water broke, a trickle beneath her skirts at first, and then a gush that puddled at her ankles on the cold, dirty ground.

"Why did you tell me?" said Annie. "I asked, but you needn't have answered. You could have kept running. Your exit was right there in front of you. Why did you tell me?"

"It's what I do," said the crone, clutching one of Annie's hands between both of her own. "It's what I've always done. It's what, I guess, I always will do."

"But why?" asked Annie, as the labor began.

"Because," said the crone, "as hard as I've tried—and believe me, Annie, I *have* tried—as hard as I've tried, I have never been able to say no to those I love."

❧

AFTER ANNIE SILVER was safely delivered of her daughter, her body was safely delivered of its soul.

The crone stood over the corpse with the baby in her arms, watching the denouement of her granddaughter's life play out just the same as it had in her vision. From the bar's back door, which had remained silent and shut through her cries for help and through the blood-curdling screams her pointless ministrations had brought forth from the dying mother—from that back door emerged the hooded figures who had pointed Annie toward her oblivion.

"It's done," said one of them.

"I'll try again," said the crone.

"No," said another of the hooded figures. "You won't."

The crone squinted and peered beneath the shadowy folds of that figure's hood. And for the first time in all these years they'd known each other, she saw a smile there.

⚜

THE CRONE CARRIED the baby back up Beacon Hill, coming to a stop in front of the family's city house and staring up at the still-lit window of the library where she and her cousins had played as children so long ago. She could see Silas pacing up there now, a scholar in silhouette, his nose buried in some old tome or another. And the crone longed to join him, to be with the man she'd loved a lifetime ago. But how could she explain to him, how could she *begin* to explain where she'd been all these years, when her honesty had already cost him so much?

She set the baby down upon the doorstep, a note tucked into its swaddling blanket with the name Annie had selected in her final moments. Then the crone rapped the heavy knocker against the door three times, said goodbye to baby Dorothy, and fled across the common once more.

❧ 9 ❧

ONE LAST BOUNTY

1915

You watch the crone flee across the common and try to find, in her stoop-shouldered gait, any trace of the girl you loved an age ago. In the tangles of silver that fly out from beneath her hood, you search for a hint of the ginger locks you used to bury your face in on Sunday afternoons after church. But, though you see nothing in this woman to make you sure that it is her, the voices on the wind have never steered you wrong before.

"The crone must die so that the horror might end." That's what they're telling you now. And so, you try to think of her as one last bounty. It's a job, you tell yourself. Nothing more, nothing less.

You raise your rifle and you take aim, sure that the kickback will take out what little shoulder you have left. And though you have no idea how your cousin's death will stop the deaths of your brother's wives, you know that it's up to you—that it's always been up to you—to see through what you long ago should have seen through.

You listen for the objections of the final voice, the one who's always late to the party, the one who's always begging for mercy, but she stays silent. For once.

And so: you take aim, Sarah. For the last time. And you fire.

ACKNOWLEDGEMENTS

"The Boot" was originally performed as a stage play at the Players' Ring in Portsmouth, New Hampshire as part of their first ever *Evening of Grand Guignol*, which ran from July 6–15, 2012. Silas was played by Chuck Galle and Ada was played by Erika Wilson. "The Boot" was later published in prose form on Clarkwoods.com.

"Animals" was first published, in slightly different form, in the anthology *Live Free or Ride: Tales of the Concord Coach* (Plaidswede Publishing, 2016).

"Cacophony," "The Patience for Taming," "The Charity of Ruin," "The Best Thing for Both of Us," "The Whore of Harwich," and "The Crone on the Common" were first published, in slightly different form, on Clarkwoods.com.

ABOUT THE AUTHOR

E. Christopher Clark is the author of the Stains of Time series, a family saga with a hint of magical realism and a whole lot of time travel. His other books include the short story collections *Out of the Woods* and *Under the World*, the novella *The Seven Wives of Silver*, and a collection of poems cheekily titled *Bad Poetry Night*. His short stories have been published in *Live Free or Ride: Tales of the Concord Coach*, *River Muse: Tales of Lowell & the Merrimack Valley*, and the University of Hawaii's *Vice-Versa*. A graduate of Lesley University's MFA in Creative Writing program, he lives in Massachusetts with his wife and daughters.

echristopherclark.com

[f] facebook.com/eccbooks
[X] x.com/eccbooks
[O] instagram.com/eccbooks
[g] goodreads.com/eccbooks
[P] pinterest.com/eccbooks
[a] amazon.com/E.-Christopher-Clark/e/B00H0G94T0